Mr Scruff

SIMON JAMES

WALKER BOOKS
AND SUBSIDIARIES

LONDON • BOSTON • SYDNEY • AUCKLAND

First published 2019 by Walker Books Ltd
87 Vauxhall Walk, London SE11 5HJ

1 3 5 7 9 10 8 6 4 2

© 2019 Simon James

The right of Simon James to be identified as author/illustrator
of this work has been asserted by him in accordance with
the Copyright, Designs and Patents Act 1988

This book has been typeset in Minion

Printed in China

British Library Cataloguing in Publication Data: a catalogue record
for this book is available from the British Library

ISBN 978-1-4063-8385-0

www.walker.co.uk
www.simonjamesbooks.com

This is Polly

she belongs to Molly.

This is Eric

he belongs to Derek.

This is Martha

she belongs to Arthur.

But who's this?

It's Mr Scruff...

For Mr Scruff there's no one.

This is Mick

he belongs to Rick.

And this is Lawrence

he belongs to Florence.

But things are looking rough,
for poor old Mr Scruff.

Wait a minute! Who's this...?

It's Jim!

They seem to like each other.

"But Jim," says Dad,
"are you sure?
 He's so BIG
 and you're so small!
 I can't see it working.
 No, not at all!"

"He's so OLD," says Mum,
"and you're so young.
 Surely a puppy would
 be more fun?"

"No," says Jim.
"He needs a home.
  A place to call his very own.
  That's what he needs.
  And that's enough
  for me –
  and Mr Scruff."

So, while
Polly has Molly,
Eric has Derek,
Martha has Arthur,
Mick has Rick,
Lawrence has Florence,
now …
Mr Scruff belongs to Jim!

And though it doesn't rhyme,
it's all worked out just fine.

But, wait a minute. Who's this...?

It's Mr Gruff.
He's come to choose a dog.

Here's a little pup.
They seem to like each other...

"I'm so BIG,
and you're so small.
But that doesn't matter.
No, not at all!"

Mr Gruff is happy.
It's the perfect
dog for him.

Can you guess the puppy's name?
Well, of course –

it's Tim!

The End